SHANNA'S Ballerina SHOW

by **Jean Marzollo**

Illustrated by **Shane W. Evans**

JUMP AT THE SUN
HYPERION BOOKS FOR CHILDREN
New York

I'm a ballerina.

**Wonder how
I know?**

I'll give you **5** clues on today's Shanna Show.

Clue 1: costume.
Leotard, tights.

**And a fancy, dancy tutu
for performing under lights.**

Clue 2: ballet shoes.
Soft, blue, and sweet.

They make me feel so la-di-da and look so pretty on my feet.

And now we find we have arrived at Clue Number 3.
You'll need to get a ticket if you want a seat to see.

You say you want to see a show?
You say you want a treat?
Admission is a penny.
Here's your ticket. Take a seat.

Clue 4: music.
Hear it sing! Hear it soar!

**Watch the movement of my arms
as I leap across the floor!**

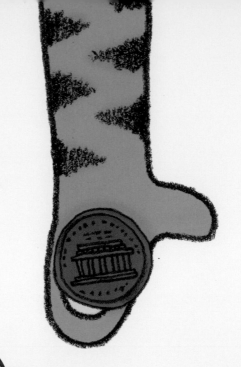

If you want a seat to see,
get a ticket: that's **3**.

Fare thee well,
it's time to go.